curious
NATURE

PLANET EARTH

QUESTIONS & ANSWERS

NANCY DICKMANN

W

FRANKLIN WATTS
LONDON • SYDNEY

First published in Great Britain in 2017 by
The Watts Publishing Group

Copyright © 2017 Brown Bear Books Ltd

All rights reserved.

For Brown Bear Books Ltd:
Text and Editor: Nancy Dickmann
Editorial Director: Lindsey Lowe
Children's Publisher: Anne O'Daly
Design Manager: Keith Davis
Designer and Illustrator: Supriya Sahai
Picture Manager: Sophie Mortimer

Concept development: Square and Circus/Brown Bear
Books Ltd

ISBN: 978 1 4451 5670 5

Printed in Malaysia

Franklin Watts
An imprint of
Hachette Children's Group
Part of the Watts Publishing Group
Carmelite House
50 Victoria Embankment
London EC4Y 0DZ

An Hachette UK company
www.hachette.co.uk
www.franklinwatts.co.uk

Websites
The website addresses (URLs) included in this book
were valid at the time of going to press. However,
it is possible that contents or addresses may change
following the publication of this book. No responsibility
for any such changes can be accepted by either the
author or the publisher.

CONTENTS

WHAT IS A PLANET?

We live on a planet called Earth. It is an enormous ball of rock, thousands of kilometres wide. There are oceans, deserts, forests and mountains on the surface.

A planet is a large object that travels around a star. Earth moves around a star that we call the Sun. Seven other planets travel around the Sun. There are also smaller objects called asteroids. The Sun, the planets and other space objects make up our solar system.

GAS PLANETS

Not all planets are made of rock. Some planets are made of gas or ice. Jupiter is the biggest planet in the solar system. It is made of gas. Its stripes are bands of swirling clouds.

MANY MOONS

A moon is an object that travels around a planet. Our moon goes around Earth, not around the Sun. Earth has one moon, but some planets have many more. Jupiter and Saturn have more than 60 each!

HOW FAR AWAY IS THE SUN?

The Sun is about 150 million kilometres away from Earth. It is an enormous ball of glowing gas. Deep inside it, one kind of gas turns into another. This change releases energy. Some of it is light, and some is heat. The Sun's energy travels to Earth. Without it, nothing could live on Earth.

The Sun will keep shining for billions of years. Then it will run out of fuel. It will swell up, and then fall in on itself.

AN ORDINARY STAR

The Sun is the brightest object in the sky. It is a star, just like the other stars that twinkle in the night sky. The Sun looks brighter than the other stars. That is because it is much closer to us.

TRAVELLING TO THE SUN

Flying in a jet plane would take almost **19 years!**

Imagine there were a road to the Sun. If you walked, it would take you **3,539 years!**

Riding your bike would take **1,517 years.**

Plants need the Sun's light to grow.

If you drove in a car, it would take **163 years.**

WHY CAN'T I DIG TO CHINA?

Have you ever dug a hole in your back garden? How deep did you go? You will never be able to dig all the way through the Earth. In fact, no one will!

In many places on Earth's surface, there is a layer of soil. It is several metres thick. If you dug far enough, you would hit solid rock. Underneath that is a very thick layer of hot rock. At the centre of the Earth is solid iron. No shovel can dig through that!

Land and the ocean floor are both part of Earth's crust.

THE DEEPEST HOLE

The deepest hole ever dug is in Russia. Scientists dug 12.3 kilometres into the ground. That still wasn't deep enough to reach Earth's mantle!

LAYERS OF THE EARTH

The **crust** is 5 to 50 kilometres thick. It is made of solid rock and is thin but strong, like an eggshell. We live on the crust.

The **mantle** is 2,900 kilometres thick. It is made of very hot rock. In some places, the rock is so hot that it acts like a thick liquid.

The **outer core** is made of metal. It is so hot that the metal has melted into a liquid.

The **inner core** is a ball of solid metal. It is extremely hot.

CAN EARTH'S SURFACE MOVE?

Earth's crust is made of huge 'plates' of rock. They fit together like a jigsaw puzzle. The plates float on top of the mantle. They move around, but very slowly. They move about as fast as your fingernails grow.

When two plates rub together, they can cause an earthquake. If it is a big earthquake, we can feel it on the surface. It feels like the ground is shaking.

Big earthquakes can make buildings collapse.

Most earthquakes happen in places where **two plates meet**.

Plate boundaries

HOW EARTHQUAKES HAPPEN

1. Two plates **get stuck** as they try to slide past each other.

2. The longer they are stuck, the more **pressure** builds up.

3. The plates finally move. The stored-up pressure makes them move a long way in a short time. This is an **earthquake**.

MEASURING EARTHQUAKES

Scientists use tools to measure how much the Earth moves. They work out how much energy was released. They give this as a number. The higher the number, the more powerful the quake. The most powerful quake scored 9.5.

WHY DO VOLCANOES ERUPT?

A volcano is a place where melted rock comes up from underground. The melted rock is called magma. Magma is lighter than solid rock. It rises towards the surface. When it rises, it creates pressure. When a volcano erupts, the magma is forced out.

Volcanoes often form along the edges of Earth's plates. Many volcanoes are cracks in the Earth's surface. Other volcanoes are mountains.

Magma is called lava once it erupts onto the surface.

WHAT COMES OUT OF A VOLCANO?

Clouds of **ash** come out of a volcano. The ash can fall like snow.

Some volcanoes shoot out **solid rocks**.

Hot **gases** come out when a volcano erupts. Water vapour is the most common gas. Deadly gases are released, too.

MUD VOLCANOES

Some volcanoes shoot out mud. They don't produce lava, so they are not true volcanoes. The mud forms when hot water from deep underground mixes with dirt or other materials.

Sometimes **melted rock** comes out of a volcano. It can shoot up into the sky, or ooze down the side. When it cools, it gets hard.

WHERE DO FOSSILS COME FROM?

Fossils are what remains of plants and animals that died long ago. Some fossils are body parts. Some are impressions left in rock, like the shape of a leaf. When a living thing dies, most of its soft parts rot away. The hard parts can get preserved in rock as fossils.

Scientists have found fossils of dinosaur bones. There are fossils of seashells, plants and eggs. They show us what animals and plants were like long ago.

Fossils of footprints can show us how dinosaurs walked.

NOT JUST BONES

Many fossils are body parts, but some are not. Scientists have found fossils of dinosaur footprints. There are even fossils of dinosaur poo!

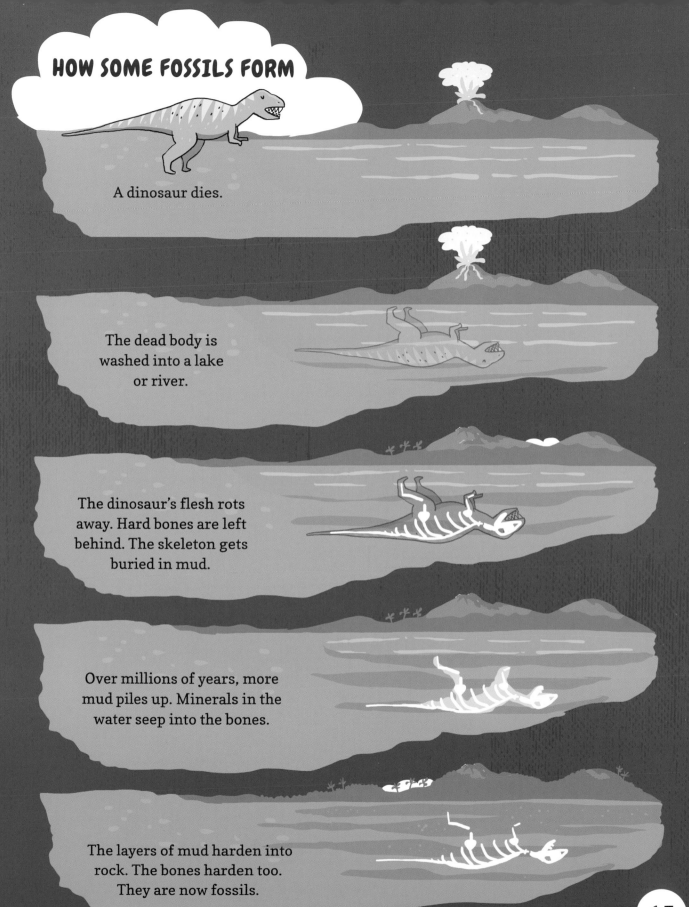

HOW SOME FOSSILS FORM

A dinosaur dies.

The dead body is washed into a lake or river.

The dinosaur's flesh rots away. Hard bones are left behind. The skeleton gets buried in mud.

Over millions of years, more mud piles up. Minerals in the water seep into the bones.

The layers of mud harden into rock. The bones harden too. They are now fossils.

15

WHERE DOES THE SUN GO AT NIGHT?

When the Sun sets, it seems to disappear. But it is just on the other side of the Earth, where you can't see it. When the Sun goes down, it is night on your side of the planet. For someone standing on the other side of the Earth, it is daytime. They can see the Sun in the sky.

The Earth spins around and around. It makes a complete circle once every 24 hours. This movement makes the Sun seem to travel across the sky.

When the Sun goes down, the sky changes colour.

DAYTIME MOON

We only see the Sun during the day. But the Moon can appear at night or in the day! The Moon travels around the Earth. From where you are, you can see it about half the time. It is very bright at night, but less bright during the day.

DAY AND NIGHT

The Sun sends out light and heat in all directions.

You

Sometimes the part of Earth that you are on is facing the Sun. It is daytime for you. On the other side of the planet, it is night.

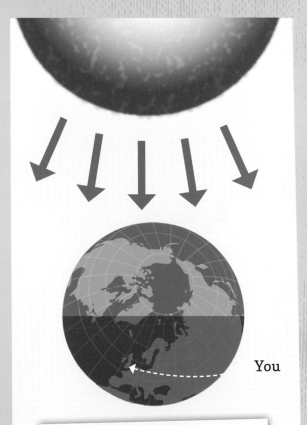

You

When your part of the Earth faces away from the Sun, it is night for you.

WHAT IS AIR MADE OF?

You cannot see air. You cannot feel it, either. But the air around us is made up of tiny particles of gas. The gas particles are much too small to see or feel.

Air is a mixture of different gases. The main one is nitrogen. There is oxygen, too. Animals need oxygen to breathe. Air also has water vapour. This is water in the form of a gas.

AIR POLLUTION
Sometimes other substances get into the air. This is called pollution. Dust, germs and harmful gases can cause air pollution. Breathing polluted air can cause health problems.

Most weather is in the lower levels of the atmosphere.

THE ATMOSPHERE

The air that surrounds Earth is called the atmosphere.

The atmosphere is about 480 kilometres thick. At the top, the air is too thin to breathe.

The **atmosphere** has different layers.

The weight of the air presses down on us. This is called **air pressure**.

Plants need air. They take in carbon dioxide gas from the air. They give out oxygen.

19

WHY DOES THE SEA GO IN AND OUT?

Sometimes the sea is a long way out, making a beach look big. At other times, the water comes further in, covering the sand. These changes happen because of tides.

Tides are made by the Moon. Every object in space pulls on objects around it. The bigger an object is, the stronger its pull. This pull is called gravity. The Moon's gravity affects the ocean. This causes tides.

TIDE POOLS

Many beaches have tide pools. These rocky areas are covered with water during high tide. At low tide, they are exposed. Plants and animals must be able to survive these different conditions.

Starfish often live in tide pools.

HOW THE MOON MAKES TIDES

The Moon's gravity pulls on the Earth. It makes the ocean's waters bulge. This part of the Earth has a **high tide.**

Between the two bulges, the water is lower. This is **low tide.**

On the opposite side, there is another **high-tide bulge.**

The Moon travels around the Earth. At the same time, the Earth spins. This makes the areas of high tide move.

HOW DEEP IS THE OCEAN?

Near the coast, the ocean is shallow. Further out, it gets deeper. The deepest point is in the Mariana Trench. It is nearly 11,000 metres deep. That's deeper than Mount Everest is tall.

The deeper you go in the ocean, the darker it gets. The water gets colder, too. The huge weight of the water above presses down.

Deep **trenches** cut through the ocean floor in some places.

THE OCEAN FLOOR

Most of the ocean floor is **flat** and deep.

DEEP-SEA EXPLORERS

Scientists have been to the deepest part of the ocean. They travel in special vehicles. These vehicles are very strong. They protect their passengers from the crushing pressure.

This vehicle is called Alvin. It can dive to 4,500 metres.

Sometimes volcanoes grow so tall that they reach the surface. They are now **islands**.

At the edge of a land mass, the ocean is **shallow**.

There are many cone-shaped **volcanoes** under the sea.

Further out, the ocean floor **slopes** steeply down.

WHERE DO RIVERS GO?

Many rivers start as small streams, high in the mountains. They flow downhill and join up with other streams. Rain and melting snow add more water. Eventually the stream becomes a large river. The river keeps flowing until it empties into the sea. Rivers are an important part of the water cycle.

GORGES

As rivers flow, they wear away the ground around them. Over many years, they can carve deep grooves in the rock. These are called gorges or canyons. Some are thousands of metres deep.

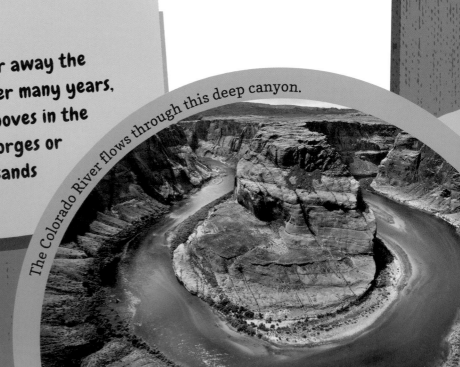

The Colorado River flows through this deep canyon.

THE WATER CYCLE

The **Sun** heats the Earth's surface.

High in the sky, the water vapour forms **clouds**.

Water in oceans, rivers and lakes warms up. It evaporates and rises into the air as **water vapour**.

Water falls from the clouds as **rain**. It falls on the oceans and the land.

On land, some of the water flows into **rivers**. The rivers take it to the ocean. The cycle begins again.

WHO LIVES ON PLANET EARTH?

We do! There are more than 7 billion people on Earth. People live in villages, towns and cities. Some live in warm places, and some in cold places.

We share our planet with other living things. Plants and animals live in almost every corner of the Earth. They live in many different biomes. A biome is a large area with similar weather and land.

LIFE ON OTHER PLANETS?

So far, Earth is the only place we know that has life. However, there may be life on other planets or moons. One day we may discover it!

More than half of the Earth's people live in busy cities.

26

THE WORLD'S BIOMES

Deserts are very dry. They are usually hot, too. Plants and animals here must find and store water.

Trees grow thick and tall in a **forest**. Many animals live in their branches.

Fish, whales and many other creatures live in **water**.

It is cold and snowy in the **polar regions**. Animals here have thick fur to keep them warm.

Grasslands have grass but few trees. Animals graze on their grasses.

Mountain slopes can be barren and rocky. Trees grow on the lower slopes.

MAKE A SUNDIAL

The Sun makes shadows on the ground. As the Sun moves across the sky, the shadows move, too. You can use these shadows to tell the time. All you need is a sundial.

WHAT YOU NEED

* paper plate
* plastic straw
* sharpened pencil
* pen or marker
* ruler
* clock or watch

1 Use the pencil to make a hole in the centre of the plate. Write a '12' on the edge of the plate. Use the ruler to draw a line from the number to the centre.

2 Push the straw into the hole. Slant it slightly towards your line.

Sundials will only work if they are positioned properly.

3 Wait for a dry, sunny day. Take your sundial outside at noon. Turn it until the straw's shadow points to the 12.

4 Make sure that the plate can't move around. (You could use some stones or other weights to hold it in place.)

5 At 1 pm, make a mark where the shadow falls. Label it '1'.

6 Every hour, mark the new time. Continue the next morning until you get back to noon.

TELLING THE TIME
Over the next few weeks, check your sundial against a clock. How accurate is it?

GLOSSARY

atmosphere layers of gases that surround the Earth

core very centre of something

crust thin outer layer of the Earth. It is made of hard rock.

energy ability to do work

erupt break or burst out suddenly. Lava can erupt from a volcano.

evaporate turn from a liquid into a gas

fossil remains of a living thing from a long time ago that are trapped in rock

gas form of matter that is not solid or liquid

gravity force that pulls objects towards each other. On Earth, gravity pulls everything down towards the ground.

magma hot, melted rock underground

mantle layer of the Earth between the crust and the core

mineral non-living substance that is formed in the Earth

moon large natural object that travels around a planet

oxygen gas in the air that living things need

particle very tiny piece of something

plate boundaries places where the plates of Earth's crust meet

preserved kept in its original state

pressure force of something pushing

star huge ball of glowing gas in space. The Sun is a star.

tides rising and falling of sea levels caused by the Moon

volcano opening in Earth's crust that lets out gases and melted rock

water vapour water that is in the form of gas

FURTHER RESOURCES

BOOKS

100 Facts Planet Earth, Peter Riley
(Miles Kelly, 2014)

Discover and Share: Planet Earth, Angela Royston
(Franklin Watts, 2015)

Fact Cat The Earth, Alice Harman
(Wayland, 2015)

Our Solar System Earth, Mary-Jane Wilkins
(Wayland, 2016)

Over 1000 Fantastic Earth Facts
(Miles Kelly, 2011)

WEBSITES

www.bbc.co.uk/education/topics/zkbbkqt
BBC Bitesize Key Stage 2 science, with short video clips
and learner guides about Earth and the solar system, day
and night, and seasonal changes.

www.dkfindout.com/uk/earth
DK Find Out! interactive pages have information on
planet Earth, volanoes and earthquakes, the water cycle,
day and night, and photographs of Earth from space.

spaceplace.nasa.gov/menu/earth/
NASA Space Place has games, activities and short video
clips about Earth and its atmosphere, weather and
oceans, the Sun and the solar system.

INDEX